Anne of
Green Gables

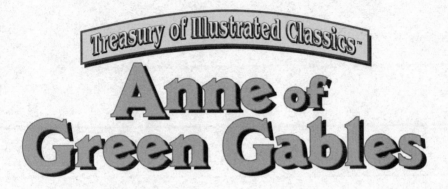

Anne of Green Gables

by
L. M. Montgomery

Adapted by
Adam Grant

Illustrated by
Lotus Do Brooks

Modern Publishing
A Division of Unisystems, Inc.
New York, New York 10022

Series UPC: 39360

Cover art by Nick Backes

Copyright ©1999, 2001, 2002 Kidsbooks, Inc.
230 Fifth Avenue
New York, New York 10001

This edition published by Modern Publishing,
a division of Unisystems, Inc.

Printed in Italy

Contents

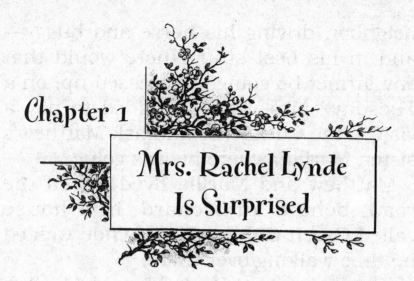

Chapter 1

Mrs. Rachel Lynde Is Surprised

Mrs. Rachel Lynde liked to sit in her kitchen window, look out over her little road, and keep an eye on everybody that passed. If she saw anything that seemed odd or out of place, she would not rest until she found out what was going on.

One afternoon in June, Mrs. Lynde was greeted with an unexpected sight.

"Isn't that Matthew Cuthbert going down the road?" she asked herself.

Sure enough, there was her closest

neighbor, driving his horse and buggy—and in his best suit! Where would that shy farmer be going, all dressed up, on a Tuesday? Mrs. Lynde decided to pay a visit to the Cuthberts' and ask Matthew's sister, Marilla, where he was going.

Matthew and Marilla lived far off the road, behind an orchard, in a house called Green Gables. Mrs. Lynde wasted no time walking over there.

"Good evening, Rachel," said Marilla. "How is everyone at your house?"

Marilla was a tall, thin woman built with all angles and no curves. She was stern and practical. But those who knew her well said that deep down inside, she almost had a sense of humor.

"We're all fine, Marilla," said Mrs. Lynde. "I was afraid that you weren't, though, when I saw Matthew riding by. I was afraid he was going for the doctor."

"Oh, I'm quite well," said Marilla. "Matthew's just gone to the train station at Bright River. We're adopting a little

boy from the orphanage in Nova Scotia. He's coming on the train tonight."

If Marilla had said that Matthew had gone to the station to meet a kangaroo from Australia, Mrs. Lynde could not have been more surprised. "A—are you serious, Marilla?"

"Of course," said Marilla, as if adopting orphan boys was something she did every Tuesday afternoon. "Last Christmas, Mrs. Spencer told us that she was going to the orphanage to get herself a little girl this spring. Matthew and I decided to have her pick up a little boy for us. Matthew is almost sixty years old now, and we could use some help around the farm."

"Well," Mrs. Lynde told the rosebushes as she walked home, "I feel sorry for that orphan. Marilla and Matthew Cuthbert don't know the first thing about raising a child. My, but I pity that little boy indeed."

If, at that very moment, she had seen the orphan waiting at the station, her pity would have been much deeper.

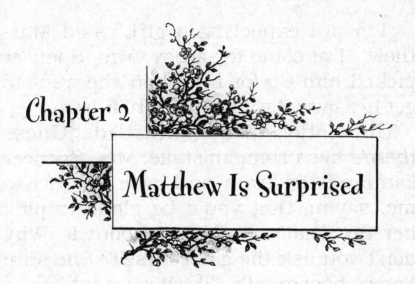

Chapter 2

Matthew Is Surprised

When Matthew Cuthbert pulled into the train station, there was no sign of a train—or any orphan boy, for that matter. As Matthew tried to figure his next move, the station master walked by.

"Any sign of the five-thirty train?" Matthew asked hopefully.

"The five-thirty has been here and gone," said the station master. "But the little girl who was dropped off for you is sitting on a bench over there, waiting for you."

"I'm not expecting a girl," said Matthew. "I've come for a boy. Mrs. Spencer picked him up for me when she went to get her own. I was to meet him here."

The station master whistled. "Guess there's been some mistake. Mrs. Spencer came off the train and gave the girl to me, saying that you'd be along to pick her up. That's all I know about it. Why don't you ask the girl yourself? She sure knows how to talk, I'll tell you that."

Matthew looked around sadly, as if maybe someone would magically appear and help him. When no one did, he went and found the girl.

She was a little thing of about eleven. She wore a very ugly dress of yellow-whitish cotton. From under a wide-brimmed, straw hat flowed two very thick braids of very red hair. Her skin was white with many freckles. Her eyes looked green in some lights, and gray in others.

Matthew was a shy man—doubly shy when it came to talking to women. In

fact, they may never have met at all if the little girl had not held out her hand and said, "I guess you're Mr. Matthew Cuthbert of Green Gables. I'm very glad to see you. I was starting to worry that you weren't coming. I had already decided that if you didn't come, I'd sleep in that big cherry tree down there. But I wouldn't have been frightened, because I would have known that you were coming to get me in the morning."

Matthew shook her little hand while she talked some more, and smiled as best as he could. He was still pretty nervous. He didn't know how he would ever explain to her that she was supposed to be a boy—especially if she never stopped talking. Finally, he decided that he would wait and explain the situation once they were safely back at Green Gables.

"I'm sorry I was late," he said shyly. "Come along. The horse is waiting."

All the way back to Green Gables, the

little girl, whose name was Anne, talked and talked.

"This just might be the most beautiful place in the whole world," she said, looking around her. "I'm going to call that pond over there the Lake of Shining Waters. Isn't that a lovely name? It's so romantic. Oh, it seems so wonderful that I'm going to live with you and belong to you. I've never belonged to anyone. The orphanage was the worst. There was no room for imagination there."

Matthew just sat and listened. She sure could talk. The first time that Anne came up for air, she noticed how quiet Matthew was being.

"Would you rather that I didn't talk?" she asked. "If you say so, I'll stop. I can stop when I make my mind up to do it, although it is very hard."

Matthew smiled. Like most quiet folks, he liked talkative people, especially if they were willing to do most of the talking themselves.

"You can talk as much as you like," he said. "I don't mind."

"Oh, I'm so glad," replied the little girl. "I know that you and I are going to get along together just fine. People laugh at me because I use such big words. But if you have big ideas, you have to use big words to express them, don't you think?"

That's how they rode together, all the way back to Green Gables.

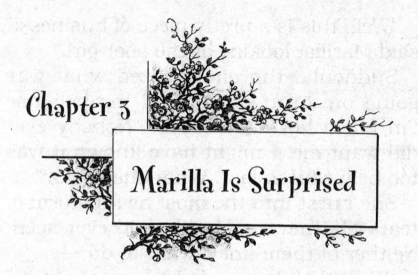

Chapter 3

Marilla Is Surprised

When Marilla heard Matthew open the front door, she ran to greet him and the new boy. But when she saw the skinny, little, red-haired girl, she stopped short.

"Matthew Cuthbert, who is that?" she demanded. "Where is our boy?"

"There wasn't any boy," he said fearfully. "There was only her. Mrs. Spencer must have made a mistake. But I couldn't just leave her there."

"Well, this is a pretty piece of business!" said Marilla, looking at the poor girl.

Suddenly, the girl realized what was going on. "You don't want me because I'm not a boy!" she cried. "Nobody ever did want me. I might have known it was too beautiful to last. What shall I do?"

She burst into the most awful storm of tears Matthew or Marilla had ever seen. Neither of them knew what to do.

"Well, there's no need to cry about it," said Marilla.

"Oh, yes there is," said the little girl.

"You would cry, too, if you were an orphan and had come to a place that you thought would be home and found out they didn't want you because you weren't a boy. It's the most tragical thing that ever happened to me."

A faint hint of a smile crept onto Marilla's face, something that she could not remember happening in a long time.

"Well, don't cry anymore. We're not going to turn you out tonight," she said. "You'll have to stay here until we can figure out what to do. What's your name?"

"Won't you please call me Cordelia?" the child asked eagerly.

"Is that your name?"

"No, but I would love to be called Cordelia! It's such an elegant name."

"I don't understand," said Marilla. "If Cordelia isn't your name, what is?"

"It's Anne Shirley," said the girl reluctantly. "But I hate it. It's *so* unromantic."

"Unromantic, fiddlesticks!" said Marilla. "Anne is a good, sensible name. There's no reason to be ashamed of it."

"If you're going to call me Anne, can you at least call me Anne spelled with an *e*? I think Anne spelled *A-n-n-e* is so much more romantic than plain old *A-n-n*."

Eventually, Marilla managed to get part of a very unromantic dinner into Anne's stomach and pack her into the little bed they had set up in one of the gable rooms upstairs. When Anne was safely asleep, Marilla came back downstairs to talk with Matthew.

"Well, this is a pretty kettle of fish,"

she said as she sat down. "One of us will have to drive over to Mrs. Spencer's in the morning and have this little girl sent back to the orphanage."

"I suppose so," said Matthew sadly. "But she is a real nice little thing."

"You don't mean to say you think we ought to keep her! What good would she be to us?"

"We might be some good to *her*," said Matthew.

"Matthew Cuthbert, I believe that child has bewitched you. I see that I'm going to have to take her back myself! I don't want an orphan girl. And if I did, I wouldn't have chosen one who can't stop talking. She must be sent back immediately."

That was the end of their conversation. Marilla, frowning, went into the kitchen to wash the dishes. Meanwhile, upstairs, a lonely, friendless child cried herself to sleep.

Chapter 4

Anne Tells Her Story

Early the next morning, Marilla and Anne were on their way to Mrs. Spencer's house. Anne, as usual, was talking about anything and everything.

"I've made up my mind to enjoy all the beautiful things we pass on this drive," she said. "Wouldn't it be nice if roses could talk? And isn't pink the most bewitching color? I do so wish that my hair weren't red. It's so unbecoming. Have you ever known anyone whose hair was red when they were young, but changed color when they grew up?"

"No, I don't think I ever have," said Marilla dryly.

Anne sighed. "Well there's another hope gone. My life is a perfect graveyard of buried hopes. That's a sentence I read in a book once, and I say it to comfort myself when I'm unhappy. It sounds so romantic, as if I were a heroine in a book."

"Since you're clearly bent on talking the entire drive," said Marilla, "tell me what you know about yourself."

"What I know about myself isn't very interesting," said Anne. "Why don't you let me tell you what I imagine about myself?"

"I don't want any of your imaginings. Just stick to the facts. Where were you born, and how old are you?"

"I was eleven last March," said Anne with a sigh. "I was born in Nova Scotia. My parents both died of fever when I was just three months old. Since then, nobody has ever really wanted me. I lived

with Mrs. Thomas for eight years, help-ing to take care of her children. But then Mr. Thomas died, and they couldn't keep me anymore. I went to live with Mrs. Hammond and took care of her eight children. She had three sets of twins! I used to get so tired carrying them about.

"After two years, Mr. Hammond died too, and the children went to live with rel-atives in the States. I had to go to the orphanage in Hopetown. They didn't want me either because they were crowded. But they *had* to take me. I was there for four months until Mrs. Spencer got me yesterday, and that's the whole story."

"Didn't you ever go to school?" demanded Marilla.

"Not very much," said Anne. "But I can read well, and I know ever so many pieces of poetry by heart."

"Were Mrs. Thomas and Mrs. Hammond good to you?" asked Marilla.

"Oh, they meant to be good and kind," answered Anne carefully. "But Mrs. Hammond had such a very hard time, what with three sets of twins . . . ."

They rode quietly for a time. Marilla began to think of what a sad story Anne's life had been so far. Maybe the decent thing to do would be to keep her. She knew that was what Matthew wanted.

A short time later, they came to Mrs. Spencer's house and Marilla remembered why they were there.

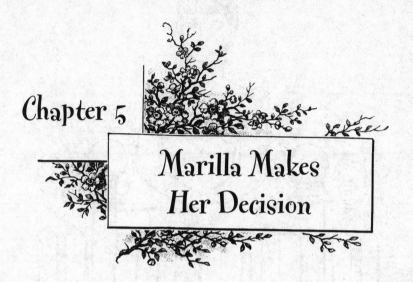

Chapter 5

Marilla Makes Her Decision

"**D**ear, dear, you're the last people I expected to see today!" said Mrs. Spencer, greeting Marilla and a sad-looking Anne at the gate. "How are you, Anne?"

"As well as can be expected, thank you," replied Anne.

Marilla explained why they had come. Mrs. Spencer was shocked, and very embarrassed at the mistake.

"Luckily, we won't have to send her back to the orphanage," said Mrs.

Spencer, brightly. "Mrs. Blewett was here just a few hours ago, saying that she wished she had a little girl to help her with the children. Anne would be just right for her. What a stroke of luck!"

Marilla didn't see anything lucky about it. Mrs. Blewett was known all over town as the stingiest woman on Prince Edward Island, and as a slave driver to all the girls who had worked for her in the past. Marilla could not imagine handing little Anne over to such a woman.

"Well, look!" exclaimed Mrs. Spencer. "Here comes Mrs. Blewett now."

Sure enough, Mrs. Blewett was coming up the walk to the Spencer house. Anne looked at the sharp-faced woman and felt as if she were going to cry.

As Mrs. Spencer explained everything to Mrs. Blewett, Mrs. Blewett's eyes darted over Anne from head to foot.

"You don't look as if there's much to you," she said. "But I suppose you'll do. You'll have to earn your keep, though."

She looked at Marilla. "I'll take her off your hands, Miss Cuthbert. If you like, I can take her home right now."

Marilla looked at the miserable expression on Anne's pale face. She began to have the uncomfortable feeling that if she ignored that look, it might haunt her until her dying day. Besides, she simply did not like Mrs. Blewett. How could she hand a sensitive, sweet child like Anne over to such a woman?

"Well I don't know," Marilla said slowly. "I didn't say that Matthew and I had *definitely* decided to send Anne back. In fact, Matthew would like to keep her. I just came over to find out how the mistake had been made. I'd better take her home and talk it over again with Matthew. If we decide not to keep her, we'll let you know tomorrow night. Will that suit you, Mrs. Blewett?"

"I suppose it will have to," sighed Mrs. Blewett.

Anne and Marilla were back in their

buggy before Anne could figure out what was happening.

"Oh, Miss Cuthbert, did you really say that you might keep me at Green Gables?" she asked breathlessly. "Or did I just imagine it?"

"You'd better learn to control that imagination of yours if you can't tell what is real and what is not," replied Marilla.

"Nothing has been decided yet. I'll have to talk it over with Matthew."

Marilla couldn't help noticing the smile on Matthew's face when she arrived back at Green Gables with Anne that evening. When she and Matthew were milking the cows, she told him Anne's history, as well as the events of the day.

"I wouldn't give a dog I liked to that Blewett woman," said Matthew.

"I feel the same way," Marilla said. "As for keeping her ourselves, I have no idea how to bring up a girl, and I'm sure I'll make a mess of it. But I'll do my best. As far as I'm concerned, she may stay."

Matthew's face was a glow of delight. "I was hoping you'd come to see it that way," he said quietly.

"But remember, Matthew, it's me who's raising her. Don't you go interfering."

"There, there, Marilla, you can have your own way," Matthew said. "Only be as kind as you can without spoiling her."

"Don't say anything to her about it tonight," said Marilla. "If we tell her she can stay, she won't sleep a wink. My, did you ever imagine that we two old goats would adopt an orphan girl? Goodness only knows what will come of it."

Chapter 6

Good News for Anne

Marilla didn't tell Anne that she could stay at Green Gables until the next afternoon. All through her morning chores, Anne wondered what would become of her. Finally, she could stand it no longer.

"Oh, please, Miss Cuthbert," she pleaded. "Won't you tell me if you are going to send me away or not? I've tried to be patient all morning, but I cannot bear it any longer."

"Well," said Marilla, "I suppose I might

as well tell you. Matthew and I have decided to keep you. That is, if you can try to be a good girl. Why child, whatever is the matter?"

"I'm crying," said Anne, as surprised as anyone else. "I can't think why. I'm as glad as I can be."

"I suppose it's because you're all excited and worked up," suggested Marilla. "Sit down and try to calm yourself."

"What am I to call you?" asked Anne. "Will I always call you Miss Cuthbert? Can I call you Aunt Marilla?"

"No, you'll call me just plain Marilla. That's what everyone in Avonlea calls me."

"I've never had an aunt or any relative at all," said Anne dreamily. "It would make me feel like I belonged. Can't I call you Aunt Marilla?"

"No," said Marilla sharply. "I am not your aunt, and I don't believe in calling people names that don't belong to them."

"But we could *imagine* that you were my aunt."

"*I* couldn't," said Marilla grimly.

"Don't you ever imagine things as being different from what they really are?" asked Anne hopefully.

"No."

"Oh, Marilla," said Anne. "How much you miss!"

That evening after supper, after Anne had picked a bunch of apple blossoms and put them in a vase in her own little room up in the east gable, Marilla went upstairs to say good night to her.

"Oh, Marilla," Anne said. "Do you think

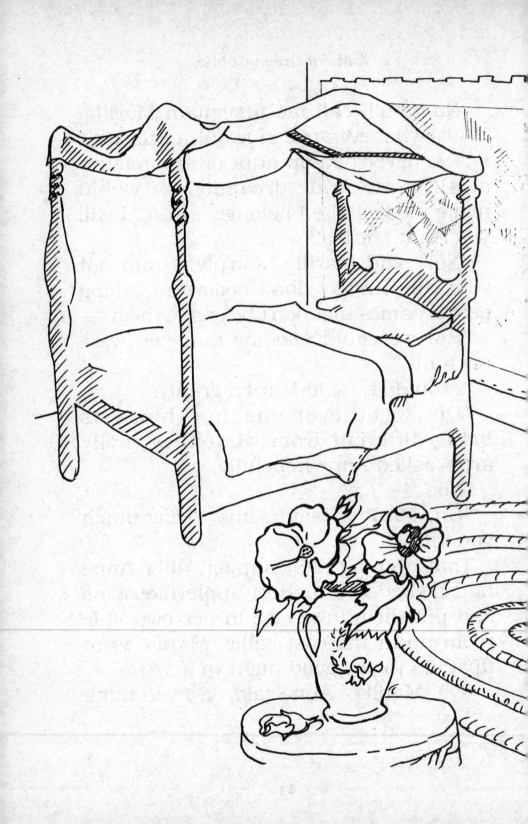

that I'll ever have a friend here in Avonlea? A real bosom friend I can tell all my deepest secrets to? I've never had one, but I've dreamed of her my whole life."

"Diana Barry lives just down the road," said Marilla. "She's about your age. Perhaps you can be playmates. But you'll have to be a very good girl at her house. Her mother is very strict."

"Diana doesn't have red hair, does she?" asked Anne. "It's bad enough to have red hair myself. I couldn't bear it in a bosom friend."

"Diana is very pretty. She has black hair and bright eyes. And she is smart and good, which is better than being pretty."

Anne was barely listening to Marilla anymore. She was lost in thought, imagining her first true bosom friend.

Chapter 7

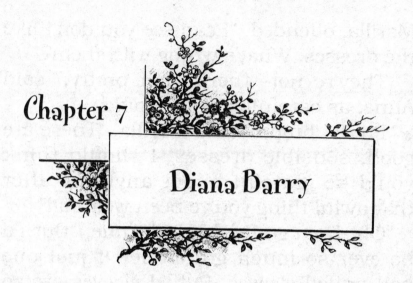

Diana Barry

"*H*ow do you like them?" asked Marilla.

Anne was looking at three new dresses spread out on her bed. Marilla had gone to the store, picked out fabric, and sewn them herself to replace Anne's plain, ugly orphanage dress. The trouble was, the new dresses were all ugly and plain, too.

"I'll imagine that I like them," said Anne, finally.

"I don't want you to imagine it," said

Marilla, offended. "I can see you don't like the dresses. What's wrong with them?"

"They're not—they're not pretty," said Anne, as carefully as she could.

"Pretty, hmph!" said Marilla. "These are good, sensible dresses. I should think you'd be grateful to get anything after that awful thing you've been wearing!"

"Oh, I *am* grateful," said Anne. "But I'd be ever so much gratefuller if just one had puffed sleeves. Puffed sleeves are so fashionable. It would give me such a thrill to wear a dress with puffed sleeves!"

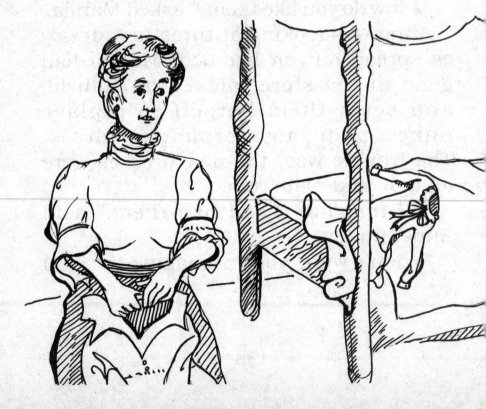

"Well, you'll have to do without your thrill," came the reply. "Now, choose the least ugly dress and put it on. I'm going to Orchard Slope to borrow a recipe from Mrs. Barry. If you'd like, you can come along and meet Diana."

"Oh, Marilla, I'm frightened," said Anne as they walked through the grove of fir trees between Green Gables and Orchard Slope. "What if Diana doesn't like me? It would be the most tragical disappointment of my life."

"Now, don't get into a fluster," said

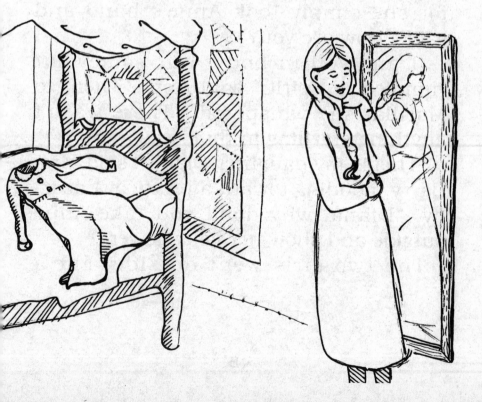

Marilla, "and stop trembling. Diana will like you fine. It's her mother you've got to worry about. If she doesn't like you, it won't matter how much Diana does. Just be polite and behave yourself."

"How do you do, Marilla?" asked Mrs. Barry cordially at the door. "And this is the little girl you adopted, I suppose?"

"Yes, this is Anne Shirley," said Marilla.

"Anne spelled with an *e*," gasped Anne, who, frightened as she was, wanted to be very clear on that point.

Mrs. Barry must not have heard her, for she simply took Anne's hand and said, "How are you?"

"I am well in body, but somewhat rumpled in spirit," said Anne. Then, to Marilla, she whispered, "There wasn't anything startling in that, was there?"

"This is my daughter Diana," said Mrs. Barry, nodding toward a pretty girl near-by. "Diana, why don't you take Anne outside and show her your flowers?"

The two girls went outside. For a

while they stood bashfully gazing at Diana's beautiful columbines, daffodils, Scotch roses, peonies, and others. Usually, a garden this lovely would have excited Anne to distraction. But today, she was too anxious. Finally, she almost whispered, "Oh, Diana, do you think you could like me enough to be my bosom friend?"

Diana laughed. She always laughed

before she spoke.

"Why I guess so," she said. "I'm so glad you've come to live at Green Gables. There are no other girls who live close by, and my sisters are all too young."

Anne took Diana's hands and they swore an oath to be friends forever.

"You're a strange girl," said Diana. "I'd heard that you were strange, but I believe I'm going to like you real well."

When it was time for Marilla and Anne to go home, Diana went with them halfway. The two girls walked with their arms around each other. After they had parted, Marilla asked Anne, "Well, did you find Diana to be a kindred spirit?"

"Oh, yes," sighed Anne, unaware that Marilla was teasing her a little. "I'm the very happiest girl on Prince Edward Island at this moment."

When they got home, Anne's cup of happiness was full to the brim—and Matthew caused it to overflow. He had just returned from town. He reached into

his pocket and handed her a small bag.

"I heard you liked chocolates, Anne. So I got you some." He smiled shyly.

"Hmph!" grunted Marilla. "It will ruin her teeth and stomach. You ought to bring her peppermints. They're healthier. Well, go ahead, Anne. You may eat them as long as Matthew has already bought them."

"I'll eat only one now, and save the rest to share with Diana tomorrow," said Anne.

Later, after Anne had gone up to her gable room, Marilla sat down, exhausted.

"I'll say this for the child," she told Matthew. "She isn't stingy. I'm glad, for I can't stand stinginess in a child. Dear me, it's only just over a week since she came, and it seems as if she's always been here."

Matthew just smiled mildly at his sister.

"Now, don't you go telling me 'I told you so,'" she shot back. "I admit that I'm glad I agreed to keep the child. And I am getting fond of her, but don't you rub it in, Matthew Cuthbert!"

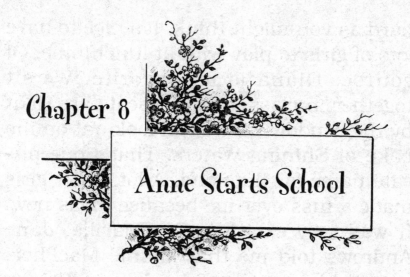

Chapter 8

Anne Starts School

Marilla was a little worried when she sent Anne off to her first day of school. How would she get along with the other children? Could she possibly keep quiet for an entire day of school?

Marilla was relieved at the end of the day, when Anne came home smiling.

"I think I'm going to like school here," Anne announced.

"I hope you were a good girl."

"I was," Anne replied. "It wasn't as

hard as you might think. It's nice to have lots of girls to play with at lunch time. Of course, Diana is my favorite. We sit together in class, and our seats are right by the window, so we can look out on the Lake of Shining Waters. That's our private name for the pond. A lot of the girls made a fuss over me because I was new. It was very exciting. Oh, Marilla, Jane Andrews told me that Minnie MacPherson told her that she heard Prissy Andrews tell Sara Gillis that I had a very pretty nose. Do I have a pretty nose? I know you'll tell me the truth."

"Your nose is well enough," said Marilla shortly. She thought that Anne's nose was very pretty, but she had no intention of telling her so. She also began to think that maybe the way Anne had managed to keep quiet all day at school was to save every word to take home and tell them to her!

Three weeks passed. Anne and Diana were the two happiest girls in Avonlea.

One crisp, September morning, they were headed to school together.

"I guess Gilbert Blythe will be in school today," said Diana. "He's been visiting his cousins all summer and he only came home Saturday. He's awfully handsome, Anne, and he teases the girls something terrible. He's also very smart. He's always been the best student in our class."

In Gilbert's absence, Anne had been the top student in class, and she had

no intention of giving up her position to anyone, not even this Gilbert Blythe.

As soon as they had sat down in class, Diana whispered to Anne, "That's Gilbert over there. Isn't he handsome?"

Anne had plenty of time to get a good look, because Gilbert was busy pinning the hair of Ruby Gillis, the girl in front of him, to the back of her seat.

Gilbert was a tall boy, with curly brown hair, hazel eyes, and a teasing smile on his face. When he saw Anne looking over at him, he looked back and winked.

"He's handsome, all right," Anne whispered to Diana, "but very fresh. It's not polite to wink at a girl you don't know."

All afternoon, while the teacher, Mr. Phillips, was helping other students, Gilbert tried to get Anne's attention. But she wouldn't look at him. He was not used to trying to attract the attention of girls in school and failing.

Finally, he reached across the aisle

and pulled one of her long, red braids. "Carrots, carrots!" he whispered loudly.

Anne sprang out of her seat with angry tears in her eyes.

"You mean, hateful boy!" she cried.

Thwack! Anne brought her writing slate down on his head and cracked it— slate, not head—straight across.

The children all fussed and laughed and whispered. Nobody had seen a scene like this at Avonlea School in

quite some time. Some of the girls even cried. Mr. Phillips went to Anne and put his hand on her shoulder.

"Anne Shirley, what does this mean?" he demanded.

Anne couldn't answer. It was too much to expect her to say in front of the whole school that she had been called "carrots." Finally, Gilbert spoke up.

"It was my fault, Mr. Phillips," he said quietly. "I teased her."

"I'm sorry to see a pupil of mine displaying such a temper and a vindictive spirit," said Mr. Phillips. "Anne, go stand on the platform in front of the blackboard for the rest of the afternoon."

Mr. Phillips took his chalk and wrote above her head, *Ann Shirley must learn to control her very bad temper.*

Anne stood and faced the class in that state of humiliation for the rest of the afternoon. As for Gilbert Blythe, she would not even so much as look at him. When school was over, she left with her red head held high. Gilbert Blythe tried to intercept her at the door.

"I'm sorry I made fun of your hair, Anne," he whispered. "Honest I am."

Anne swept past him without a word.

"I shall never forgive Gilbert Blythe," she said to Diana when they were out on the road. "And Mr. Phillips spelled my name without an *e*, too."

Little did Anne know that this was the beginning of a long and difficult relationship for her and Gilbert Blythe.

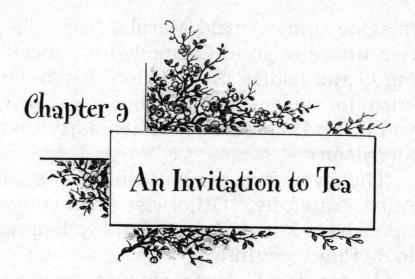

Chapter 9

An Invitation to Tea

Octber was a beautiful month at Green Gables. The birches turned as golden as sunshine, and the maples behind the orchard were royal crimson. Anne loved the world of color around her.

"Oh, Marilla," Anne shouted one Saturday morning, "I'm so glad that there's an October. Imagine how awful it would be to live in a world that went straight from September to November!"

"Young lady, you know I try never to

imagine things," said Marilla. "Now, listen. I have to go to Carmody for a meeting of the Ladies' Association. I may be crazy for suggesting this, but why don't you invite Diana here for a tea party this afternoon?"

"Then you *can* imagine things!" said Anne gratefully. "Otherwise, you could never have known how much I've longed to do that very thing!"

All day long, Anne was so excited about her tea party that she could think of nothing else. Marilla helped her plan the menu. Besides tea, they would have fruitcake, cookies, and ginger snaps, with butter and cherry preserves.

"And," said Marilla, "there is half a bottle left of raspberry cordial from the church social the other night. You may serve that, too."

"Oh, Marilla," cried Anne, "I can just imagine myself sitting down at the head of the table and pouring out the tea, just like a real lady. And asking Diana if she

takes sugar. I know she doesn't, but I'll ask her just as if I didn't know."

Later that day, Diana arrived in her second-best dress. Usually, she would just barge into the kitchen. But today, she knocked primly at the front door.

Anne let her in, and soon they were sitting at the table, making polite conversation about their families, as it is proper for grown-up women to do at tea.

"We have something delicious to

drink," said Anne. "It's bright red. I love drinks that are bright red. They taste twice as good as any other color."

As they sat and ate and drank and talked, the girls soon forgot about acting like grown-ups and started gossiping about their classmates from school. They discussed Charlie Sloan's crush on Em White, and how Ruby Gillis had charmed her warts away with a magic pebble from the creek.

After Diana's third glass of cordial, Anne left the room to fetch the tea and cake. But when she returned, she found Diana sitting with her head in her hands.

"Oh, Anne," moaned Diana. "I feel awfully sick. I think I'd better go home."

"But you can't leave without tea and cake!" cried Anne.

"I *have* to go home," repeated Diana. "I feel awfully dizzy."

Anne realized that something was really wrong. She walked Diana home, then went back to Green Gables in tears.

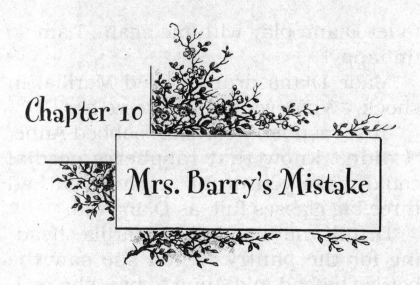

Chapter 10

Mrs. Barry's Mistake

The next day, Marilla sent Anne to Mrs. Lynde's house on an errand. But when Anne returned, she had tears running down her face.

"What's wrong now?" asked Marilla.

"Mrs. Lynde saw Diana's mother this morning," wailed Anne. "Mrs. Barry told her that I made Diana drunk yesterday and sent her home in a disgraceful condition. She said I must be a bad, wicked girl and she's never ever going to let Diana play with me again. I am so unhappy!"

"Made Diana drunk?" said Marilla, in shock. "Whatever did you serve her?"

"Just raspberry cordial," sobbed Anne. "I didn't know that raspberry cordial could make you drunk, even if you had three big glasses full, as Diana did."

"Drunk, nothing," said Marilla, heading for the pantry. When she saw the bottle she had told Anne to use, she realized the mistake. It wasn't raspberry cordial at all, but leftover homemade wine.

"Well, Anne, you certainly have a genius for getting into trouble. You went and gave Diana currant wine instead of raspberry cordial. Couldn't you tell the difference?"

"I never tasted it," sobbed Anne. "Now whatever will I do? I'll never see my bosom friend again because of this."

"There, there, child, don't cry," soothed Marilla. "It's not your fault. I told you the wrong bottle. I'm sure that Mrs. Barry will change her mind when she hears the whole story. She probably thinks you did it on purpose, as a joke. Go over to Orchard Grove and explain."

"I'm scared," admitted Anne. "I wish *you'd* go talk to her. You're so much more dignified than I am."

"Well, I will," said Marilla. "Don't cry anymore, Anne. It will be all right."

But when Marilla returned from Orchard Grove, Anne could see by the look on her face that it was *not* all right.

"Of all the unreasonable women I ever

saw, that Mrs. Barry is the worst," she said, trying to make Anne feel better. "I told her it was all a mistake. But she simply didn't believe me. Finally, I told her that neither currant wine nor raspberry cordial was meant to be gulped three glasses at a time, and that if my child was that greedy I'd sober her up with a right good spanking."

But poor Anne was crushed. She had lost her one bosom friend. That night, once again, she found herself up in her little gable room, crying herself to sleep.

Chapter 11

Anne's Days of Heartbreak

The next afternoon, Anne was bent over some needlework when she looked up and saw Diana hiding behind a bush in the yard. Anne ran out of the house and across the yard. But she could see from the sad look on Diana's face that their situation had not changed.

"Your mother hasn't changed her mind?" she asked.

"No, and she says that I'm never to play with you again," Diana replied. "I've

cried and cried and told her it wasn't your fault, but it's no use. It took me an hour of begging to get her to let me come down and say good-bye for ten minutes."

"Ten minutes isn't very long to say an everlasting farewell in," Anne said tearfully. "Oh, Diana, will you promise never to forget me, the friend of your youth?"

"Indeed I will," sobbed Diana, "and I'll never have another bosom friend. I couldn't love anybody as I love you."

"Oh, Diana," cried Anne, "you love me?"

"Sure I do. Didn't you know that?"

"No," said Anne. "I thought you liked me, of course, but I never hoped you loved me. I didn't think anyone could. No one ever has. This is a ray of light, even though it's such a sad occasion."

To mark the occasion, Anne cut a lock of Diana's hair to keep forever.

"I will always love thee, Diana," said Anne, speaking as formally as she could, through her tears. Both girls cried as Diana walked slowly back to her house.

"Well," Anne told Marilla later, "I'll never have another friend. I'm worse off than ever. In fact, I doubt I'll live very long. Maybe when Mrs. Barry sees me lying cold in my grave, she'll feel bad about what she did and let Diana come to my funeral."

"I don't think there's much fear of your dying of grief as long as you can talk, Anne," said Marilla unsympathetically.

The next day in school, Anne's heart

ached when she could no longer sit with Diana, but she felt a little comfort to be able to see her across the room. Sometime after lunch, another girl passed Anne a note. She opened the note and read it.

Dear Anne,

Mother says I'm not to play with you or talk to you even in school. It isn't my fault and don't be cross with me, because I love you as much as ever.

Your true friend,
Diana Barry

Anne read the note, quickly wrote a reply, and sent it back across the room.

My dear Diana,

Of course I'm not cross at you because you have to obey your mother! But our spirits can still be together. I shall keep my lock of your hair forever.

Yours until death do us part,
Anne or Cordelia Shirley

P.S. I shall sleep with your letter under my pillow tonight.

A. or C. S.

To fight her grief over the next days, Anne threw herself fully into competing with Gilbert Blythe for the best grades in the class. Once in a while, the two girls would look across the schoolroom at each other and sigh. This is how they spent quite a few days—then something quite remarkable happened.

Chapter 12

Anne to the Rescue

It was a cold day in January when Marilla and Mrs. Rachel Lynde went for a trip off the island and were gone overnight. It was up to Anne and Matthew to look after Green Gables.

Anne and Matthew had become very fond friends, and they were having a great time talking while Anne made dinner that night, when they heard fast footsteps on the icy porch. The next moment, in raced Diana Barry, white-faced and breathless. Anne was so shocked to see her that she dropped a whole plate of potatoes on the floor.

"Oh, Anne, do come quick," said Diana nervously. "Minnie May is sick. She's got the croup, and mother and father are away in town, and there's no one to call for the doctor. Oh, Anne, I'm so scared!"

Minnie May was Diana's three-year-old sister. Little children could die from croup if they didn't get proper treatment.

As soon as Matthew heard the news he reached for his hat and went out the door.

"He's gone to Carmody, for the doctor," said Anne, putting on her coat and scarf. "Matthew and I are such kindred spirits that I can read his thoughts."

"I don't think we can wait for the doctor," sobbed Diana. "What if he's away? Mary Joe has no idea what to do!" Mary Joe was the young woman hired by Mrs. Barry to look after the children.

"Don't cry," said Anne cheerfully. "I know exactly what to do for croup. Don't forget that I looked after Mrs. Hammond's three pairs of twins. They all got croup regularly. Just wait until I get the ipecac bottle. You might not have any at your house. Come on now, let's go!"

When they got to Diana's house, they found little Minnie May on the sofa, very sick indeed. Anne went to work quickly.

"Minnie May has the croup all right," she said. "She's pretty bad, but I've seen worse. First, we need lots of hot water. Mary Joe, you put wood in the stove. I'll give her a dose of ipecac."

Minnie May did not take the ipecac easily. But Anne had not brought up three pairs of twins for nothing. Down the ipecac went, not once but many times during the long, scary night.

It was three o'clock in the morning when Matthew arrived with a doctor. By then, he was not needed. Minnie May was much better and was sleeping soundly.

"I was awfully near giving up," Anne told the doctor. "After I'd given the last dose of ipecac, I was afraid that she might choke to death. But she started coming around right after that."

Later that morning, when the Barrys had returned, the doctor took them aside. "That little red-headed girl saved your baby's life last night," he said. "It would have been way too late by the time I got here. She's quite unusual, isn't she?"

Anne slept almost the entire next day. When she woke up, Marilla was home, standing in the kitchen with a plate of hot dinner for Anne.

"Matthew told me all about last night," she said, smiling at Anne. "It's a good thing you knew what to do. I certainly wouldn't have known."

Marilla had exciting news for Anne, but refused to tell her what it was until after dinner. Finally, as Anne put down her knife and fork, Marilla said, "Mrs. Barry was here earlier. She says that

you saved Minnie May's life, and she is
very sorry that she acted the way she
did about the currant wine mistake. She
knows that you didn't mean to make
Diana drunk, and hopes that you'll forgive her and be good friends with Diana
again. You can go over there tonight, if
you like. Now Anne Shirley, for pity's
sake, don't fly clean up into the air!"

Anne looked so excited, it almost
seemed as if she *would* fly into the air.

"Oh, Marilla," she cried. "Can I go right now?"

"Yes, yes, run along," said Marilla. "But for goodness' sake, put on your coat. It's freezing outside."

Anne came dancing back an hour later with an expression of pure delight on her little, freckled face.

"You see before you a perfectly happy person," she announced to Marilla. "When I left Diana's house Mrs. Barry asked me to come over as often as I like!"

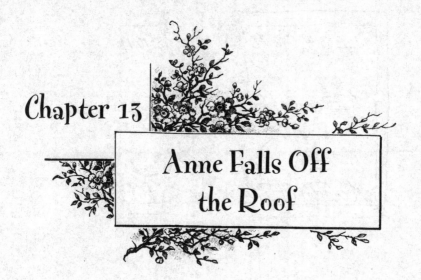

Chapter 13

Anne Falls Off the Roof

Anne and Diana went back to being best bosom friends, and sat together every day at school. Soon, over a year had passed, and many changes had come to Avonlea. Mr. Phillips had moved away and been replaced by a new teacher, Miss Stacy. Anne and the rest of the children couldn't wait to start school again with their new teacher.

As summer faded, they grew more and more restless. With nothing better to do,

they got into the habit of daring each other to do strange things.

Carrie Sloan dared Ruby Gillis to climb to the top of the tallest oak tree in town. Ruby did it, even though she was deathly afraid of the exact kind of green caterpillars that lived in oak trees. Anne dared Josie Pye to walk across the top of the Barrys' fence, which Josie did easily.

When Josie was finished, Anne crossed her arms and said, "I don't think it's so great to walk a little fence. I knew a girl in Marysville who could walk all the way around the edge of her roof."

"I don't believe it," said Josie. "Nobody could do that. You couldn't, anyhow."

"Oh, couldn't I?" asked Anne, rashly.

"Then I dare you to do it," said Josie. "I dare you to climb up there and walk all the way around the edge of Diana's roof."

Anne turned pale with fright, but there was clearly only one thing to be done. She walked toward Diana's house,

where a ladder was leaning against the side. All the girls gasped.

"Don't do it, Anne!" cried Diana. "You'll fall off and be killed! Never mind Josie Pye. It isn't fair to dare anyone to do something so dangerous."

"I must do it. My honor is at stake," said Anne quietly. "I must walk across that roof or die trying! If I am killed, I would like you to have my pearl ring."

The girls looked on in silence as Anne climbed the ladder to the roof. All she

could think of as she began her long trek around the edge was how high up she was, and that learning to walk the edge of a roof was not really a useful skill in life.

Anne managed to take several large steps before the catastrophe came. Then she swayed, lost her balance, stumbled, staggered, and fell, sliding over the roof and crashing into the bushes below. It happened so fast that all the other girls could do was give a terrified shriek.

Luckily, Anne managed to fall off the side of the roof that ran low over the end of the porch and was fairly close to the ground. When the girls ran around to that side, they found poor Anne in a little heap on the ground.

"Oh, Anne, speak to me. Just one word. Speak to me and tell me if you're killed," wailed Diana, throwing herself on her knees beside her friend.

"No, Diana, I am not killed," Anne said weakly. "But I think I am unconscious."

Just then, Diana's mother appeared on the scene. At the sight of Mrs. Barry, Anne tried to scramble to her feet, but only gave a little yelp and fell back to the ground.

"What's the matter, are you hurt?" asked Mrs. Barry.

"It's my ankle," said Anne. "Please ask Mr. Barry to carry me home, because I'm sure I cannot walk."

Marilla was out in the orchard picking apples when she saw Mr. Barry coming over the log bridge with a parade of little girls trailing after him. In his arms he carried Anne, whose head lay limp against his shoulder.

Fear stabbed Marilla to the heart, and she realized how much Anne had come to mean to her. She always knew that she liked Anne. But now, as she hurried toward the girls, she knew that Anne was dearer to her than anything on earth.

"Mr. Barry, what happened to her?"

she gasped, more shaken than she had been in years.

Anne lifted her head and spoke up. "Don't be frightened, Marilla," she said. "I was walking on Diana's roof and I fell off. I think I sprained my ankle. But Marilla, I *could* have broken my neck. Let's look on the bright side of things."

"I should have known that you'd do something like that," said Marilla, trying not to show how relieved she was. "Bring her in here and lay her on the sofa. Mercy me, the child has gone and fainted!"

The pain had finally gotten to Anne, and she fainted dead away. Matthew went for the doctor right away. It turned out that the injury was worse than they thought—Anne's ankle was broken.

That night, when the doctor had gone and Marilla was upstairs, tucking Anne into bed, Anne said to her, "Are you very sorry for me, Marilla?"

"It was your own fault," replied Marilla.

"That is just why you should feel sorry

for me. Because the thought that it is my own fault is what makes it so hard. If I could blame it on someone else, it would make me feel so much better."

It sure seemed a strange kind of logic to Marilla.

"What would *you* have done," asked Anne, "if you had been dared to walk across Diana's roof?"

"I would have stayed on firm ground and let them dare away!" crowed Marilla.

"But you have more strength of mind than I, Marilla. I couldn't bear losing to Josie Pye," said Anne sadly. "But I think I've been punished enough that you need not be cross with me. The doctor hurt me a lot when he set my ankle. I won't be able to walk for six or seven weeks and I'll miss the new teacher. She won't be new by the time I get back to school. And Gil—I mean everybody—will be ahead of me in class. Oh, I am in a terrible situation. I'll try to bear it bravely if you won't be cross with me."

"There, there, I'm not cross," said Marilla. "You're an unlucky child, there's no doubt about that. Now, try to eat some dinner."

"Isn't it lucky that I've got such an imagination?" asked Anne. "It should help me through. What do people who haven't any imagination do when they break their bones, Marilla?"

Luckily, Anne didn't have to rely on just her imagination during her seven weeks in bed. A steady stream of visitors kept her fairly well occupied.

"Everybody has been so good and kind, Marilla," sighed Anne happily on the first day that she could limp across the floor. "It isn't very pleasant being laid up, but there is a bright side to it. You find out how many friends you have! Of course Diana came to see me every day. Mrs. Allan, the minister's wife, came fourteen times. Isn't that something? Even Josie Pye came by. I was as polite as I could be because I think she was sorry that she had dared me to walk on Diana's roof. If I had been killed, she would have felt awful her whole life, Marilla."

Anne went on like this for quite some time, until finally, Marilla found a tiny space in the conversation to suggest, "There's one thing plain to be seen, and that is that your fall off the Barry roof hasn't injured your tongue at all."

Chapter 14

Matthew Insists on Puffed Sleeves

It was October when Anne was well enough to return to school. She had heard many reports about the new teacher, but she was still surprised at how well she and Miss Stacy liked each other right from the start. Anne's report cards, which had always been good, improved every week.

"I love Miss Stacy with all my heart," she told Matthew and Marilla. "When she says my name, I can tell that she's spelling it with an *e*. We recited poetry in class yesterday. You would have been proud of how I put my whole heart and soul into it."

"Maybe sometime you can recite it for me out in the barn," suggested Matthew.

"Of course I will," replied Anne.

She and Matthew had become the best of friends. When December came around and Christmas was near, Matthew wanted to do something special for her. One day as he watched her playing with her friends, he noticed that there was something that made her different from the rest of the girls. But he couldn't say what.

Then he realized what it was: Her clothes were different. All the other girls wore brightly colored dresses, but Marilla dressed Anne in dark, plain things. And Anne's sleeves were plain and straight. They didn't look anything like the puffed sleeves the others wore.

Matthew decided then and there that he would buy Anne a lovely, fashionable dress for Christmas, so she could be like the other girls. But how to go about it?

The next evening, Matthew went to town to buy the dress. He had a feeling that it was going to be difficult, and he wanted to get it over with. His shyness was bad enough at normal times, but buying a girl's dress was as unknown to him as flying to the moon.

He headed right for Samuel Lawson's store. But when he got inside and faced

Miss Harris, the charming lady at the counter, he lost all his nerve.

"What can I do for you this evening, Mr. Cuthbert?" she asked, smiling.

"Have you any—any—well, say now, any garden rakes?" asked Matthew.

Miss Harris looked a bit surprised to hear a man ask for garden rakes in the middle of December.

"I think we might have one or two left," she said. "I'll go and see."

When she returned with the rake and asked, "Anything else tonight?" Matthew, trying to be brave, replied, "Well now, if it's not too much trouble I'd like to look at—at—some sugar!"

He had failed again.

"How much sugar would you like, Mr. Cuthbert?" Miss Harris asked.

"Oh, I'll take twenty pounds of it," Matthew said, sweating a little.

Matthew hid the rake in the tool shed when he reached home. But the sugar he took in to Marilla.

"Twenty pounds of sugar?" she yelled. "Whatever made you buy so much? Have you lost your mind?"

"I—I thought it might come in handy," he suggested, making his escape.

Matthew thought it over and decided that he was going to need a woman's help. Marilla was out of the question. Matthew was sure that she would try to talk him out of it. Mrs. Rachel Lynde was the only other woman in the whole town he felt comfortable talking to. He went to see her, and she thankfully took the whole matter out of his hands.

"Pick out a dress for you to give to Anne? Of course I will!" she exclaimed. "I'll buy the fabric and make it myself. What kind would you like?"

"I don't know," he stammered. "But I think they make the sleeves differently nowadays. I'd like them made the new way—if it's not too much trouble."

"Puffed sleeves? Of course. Don't worry another minute. I'll make it in the latest fashion," replied Mrs. Lynde.

Chapter 15

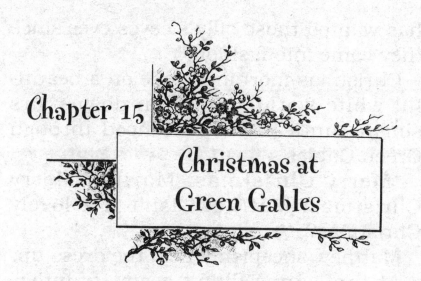

Christmas at Green Gables

Mrs. Lynde brought the new dress over on Christmas Eve.

"So this is what Matthew has been looking so mysterious over and grinning to himself about for two weeks," Marilla said. She tried not to feel insulted that Matthew had asked Mrs. Lynde to make the dress instead of her.

"There's enough material in those sleeves to make a waist!" she said. "I hope Anne will finally be satisfied. She has wanted those silly sleeves ever since they came into fashion."

Christmas morning broke on a beautiful white world. Anne ran downstairs singing until her voice echoed through Green Gables.

"Merry Christmas, Marilla! Merry Christmas, Matthew! Isn't it a lovely Christmas?"

Matthew sheepishly held the dress up.

At first, Anne didn't seem to understand. Then a huge smile broke across her face. "Is that for me?" she cried. "Oh, Matthew!"

Anne took the dress and looked at it in wonder. It was a lovely and silky brown, with all the latest tucks and pinnings. The sleeves were the best of all: long elbow cuffs with two beautiful brown puffs separated by rows of shirring and bows of brown silk ribbon.

"It's a Christmas present for you, Anne," said Matthew shyly. "Why are you crying? Don't you like it?"

Anne's eyes had filled with tears. "Like it? Oh, Matthew, it's perfectly exquisite. I can never thank you enough. It's like a happy dream!" she shouted.

"Well, let's have breakfast," interrupted Marilla. "I must say, I don't think you need the dress, Anne, but since Matthew got it for you, see that you take good care of it. Mrs. Lynde left a hair ribbon for you as well, to match the dress."

"I don't see how I'm going to eat breakfast," said Anne. "Breakfast seems so commonplace after such excitement!"

That night there was a talent show and concert at the school. Anne recited two poems and was the star of the evening.

"Oh, Diana, I was so nervous," said Anne later. "When Mr. Allan called out my name, I really don't know how I ever got on that stage. Then I thought of my lovely puffed sleeves and took courage. I had to live up to those sleeves."

"Wasn't the boys' acting fine?" asked Diana. "Gilbert Blythe was splendid.

Anne, I think it's awful the way you treat Gil. You know, when you ran off the stage, a rose fell out of your hair. I saw Gil pick it up and put it in his breast pocket. You're such a romantic, I thought you'd be pleased with that."

"It's nothing to me what that person does," sniffed Anne. "I simply never waste a thought on him."

That night, Matthew and Marilla sat up and talked by the fire after Anne went to bed.

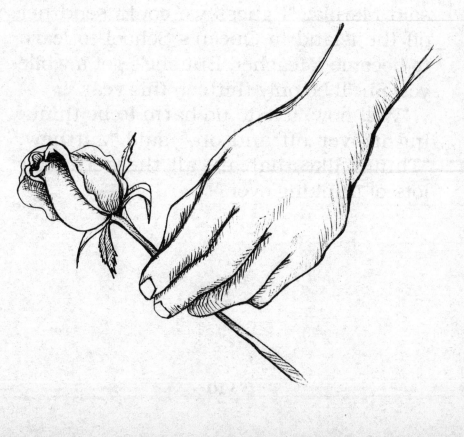

"I think our Anne did as well as any of them tonight," said Matthew proudly.

"Yes, she did," admitted Marilla. "Although I'd never tell her so—she's so vain already."

"Well now, I was proud of her and I told her so, right before she went upstairs," said Matthew. "She's a smart girl, Marilla. Sooner or later, she's going to need a better school than what we've got here in Avonlea, you know."

"I've been thinking about that, too," said Marilla. "I guess we could send her off the island to Queen's School to learn to become a teacher. But she's got a while yet. She'll be only thirteen this year."

"Well now, it'll do no harm to be thinking it over off and on," said Matthew. "Things like that are all the better for lots of thinking over."

Chapter 16

A Matter of Pure Vanity

Marilla was walking home from town on a chilly April evening, looking forward to a fire in the hearth and the dinner Anne would have waiting. She thought about how cold and drab homecomings used to be before Anne was around.

But when Marilla entered Green Gables, she was surprised to find it empty and cold. There was no briskly snapping fire, no piping-hot dinner on the table.

"I'll settle Miss Anne when she comes

home," snapped Marilla when Matthew came in from plowing. "She's off gossiping with Diana or some other nonsense. She had no business leaving the house like this after I told her to stay home this afternoon and look after things. With all her faults, I never found her disobedient or untrustworthy before. I'm real sorry to find her so now."

"Well now," said Matthew, "don't go calling her untrustworthy until you're sure that she has disobeyed you.

Maybe there's a very good explanation for this."

"She's not here when I told her to stay," Marilla snapped back. "I think she'll find it hard to explain that. I knew that you'd take her side."

It was dark by the time dinner was ready—and still no sight of Anne. After dinner, a worried Marilla went up to Anne's room to fetch a candle. When she had lit it, she turned around to find Anne lying on her own bed.

"Mercy!" said Marilla, startled. "Have you been asleep all this time, Anne?"

"No," was the muffled reply.

"Are you sick then?"

Anne moved farther away on the bed, as if she did not wish to be seen.

"No. But please, Marilla, go away and don't look at me. I'm awfully depressed, and I don't care about anything anymore because I don't think I'll be able to go anywhere ever again."

"Anne Shirley, what have you done?" asked the confused Marilla. "Get up this minute and tell me. Whatever is it?"

Finally, Anne inched slowly away from the wall and showed her face.

"Look at my hair," she whispered.

Marilla lifted her candle and looked at Anne's long hair.

"Anne Shirley, what have you done to your hair? It's green!"

Anne's hair was a strange, dull, bronzy green, with streaks of the original red here and there. Marilla had

never seen anything more hideous in her life.

"I thought nothing could be as bad as red hair," moaned Anne. "But it's ten times worse to have green hair."

"I might have expected something like this," said Marilla, when she had coaxed Anne down to the warm kitchen. "You haven't gotten into a scrape for over two months. What on earth did you do to your hair?"

"I dyed it," said Anne. "I knew it was a wicked thing to do, but I thought it was worthwhile being just a little wicked to get rid of red hair. I meant to be extra good in other ways to make up for it."

"Well," replied Marilla, "if I thought it was worthwhile to dye my hair, I would have dyed it a decent color, at least. I wouldn't have dyed it green!"

"Neither would I," protested Anne. "But the salesman assured me that it would turn my hair a beautiful raven black."

That night they scrubbed and washed Anne's poor hair until you might have thought it would fall out. But when they were finished, it was no less green than when they began.

"Oh, Marilla, what shall I do? asked Anne in tears. "People have pretty well forgotten my other mistakes, like making Diana drunk and falling off her roof. But they'll never forget this."

Anne's unhappiness lasted another week. During that time, she shampooed her hair every day and never left the house. Only Diana knew her terrible secret, and she promised never to tell.

At the end of the week, Marilla said, "It's no use, Anne. That green is there to stay. Your hair must be cut off. There's no other way. You can't go out with it looking like that."

Although the idea made Anne weep, she knew Marilla was right. She went to fetch the scissors right away.

Later, after she had cried herself out,

Anne faced the mirror. Marilla had had to cut the hair very, very short. It was not a pretty picture, to say it kindly.

"I'll never, never look at myself again until my hair grows," said Anne. But then she changed her mind. "Yes, I will, too. It will be my punishment. I will look at myself every time I pass a mirror, to remind myself of my vanity."

Anne's clipped head made quite a splash in school the next day. Nobody guessed the real reason she had cut it—not even Josie Pye, who told Anne that she looked like a scarecrow.

"I didn't say one thing when she said that to me," Anne told Marilla later, "because I consider it to be a part of my punishment, and so I should bear it patiently. I'll always remember this and never again will I try to be beautiful. It's better to be good, although sometimes that's hard to remember. Am I talking too much, Marilla? Is it making your head hurt worse?"

Marilla was lying on the sofa with one of her terrible headaches.

"My head is better now," Marilla replied softly. "But it was awful bad this afternoon. These headaches of mine are getting worse and worse. I must remember to see the doctor about them. As for your chatter, I think I've gotten used to it."

Which was Marilla's way of saying that she liked it.

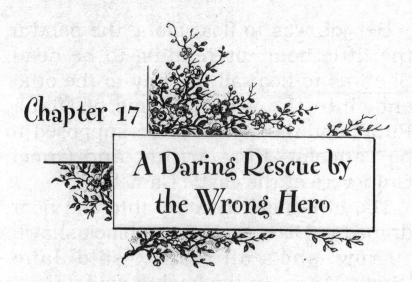

Chapter 17

A Daring Rescue by the Wrong Hero

That summer, Anne and Diana spent most of their playtime on the pond. They fished for trout from the bridge, and learned to row Mr. Barry's little flat-bottomed boat.

Sometimes, all the girls from school would come over and they would act out scenes from their favorite books. Today, they were playing "Elaine's Funeral" from the King Arthur stories. Anne was playing Elaine, the fair, dead lily maid.

Her job was to float along the pond in the little boat, pretending to be dead. She was to float all the way to the other end, into the waiting arms of Diana, Ruby, and Jane, who were supposed to be Lancelot, King Arthur, and Queen Guinevere at the castle Camelot.

The girls packed Anne into the boat, draped in Diana's mother's black shawl.

"Now, she's all ready," said Jane. "Smile, Anne. In the book it said, 'Elaine lay as though she smiled.' That's better."

Diana, Jane, and Ruby pushed the boat out onto the pond, then ran across the bridge to the far edge of the pond to wait for the fair Elaine's funeral barge. But for some reason, it didn't come.

What they hadn't seen was that as soon as "Elaine" had been cast into the pond, her barge started to leak. In just a moment, it was necessary for Anne to scramble to her feet, pick up her shawl, and check the huge crack in the bottom of the boat. Water was pouring through

it, and the little boat was about to sink. If it sank in the deepest part of the pond, she would be in serious trouble.

Where were the oars? They had left them on the bank, to make the whole thing look more romantic! Anne gave a little scream, which nobody heard. But she did not lose her courage. She had one chance—just one—to save herself.

The bridge was set on three strong tree stumps. If she could drift near enough to reach one of them, she could grab on and wait for a rescue.

Anne prayed with all her might for the little boat to drift toward the bridge. Sure enough, it did.

"The boat bumped right into one of the stumps," Anne told Matthew the next day, "and I scrambled right onto it. There I was, clinging to that slippery old log with no way of getting up or down. It was a very unromantic position, but when you have just escaped a watery grave, you don't think about those things."

The boat drifted on without her, then sank in the middle of the pond. Ruby, Jane, and Diana watched it sink, and were convinced that Anne had gone down with it. For a moment, they stood in terror. Then, shrieking at the tops of their voices, they started running frantically through the woods, never pausing as they crossed the road to look under the bridge.

Anne, clinging desperately to her precious stump, saw them all fly by. She tried to tell herself that help would soon come. But each passing minute felt like an hour, and her arms started to hurt.

Where had the girls gone? What if they had all fainted? What if help never came? Suppose she grew so tired that she could no longer hold on? Anne started imagining all kinds of horrible possibilities.

Then, just as she thought she really could not bear the ache in her arms and wrists another moment, Gilbert Blythe came rowing under the bridge!

Gilbert looked up and, much to his

amazement, saw her little white face looking down on him with big, frightened, but unfriendly eyes.

"Anne Shirley," he cried. "How on earth did you get there?"

Without waiting for an answer, he pulled close and held out his hand. Anne grasped his hand and scrambled down into his boat. She sat in the stern—cold, furious, and dripping wet.

"What happened, Anne?" asked Gilbert kindly, picking up his oars.

"We were playing Elaine," said Anne coldly, without even looking at her rescuer. "I had to drift down to Camelot in the barge—I mean, the boat. But it was leaking, so I had to climb onto the stump before it sank. Would you be kind enough to row me to the landing?"

Gilbert rowed to the landing where Anne, refusing help, hopped ashore. "Thank you very much," she said as she turned away. But Gilbert, who had also climbed ashore, grabbed her hand.

"Anne," he said. "Look here. Can't we be friends? I'm very sorry that I made fun of your hair that time. I didn't mean to hurt you. It was only for a joke. Besides, it was long ago. I think your hair is really pretty now, honest. Let's be friends."

For a moment Anne stopped. She had a new odd feeling that Gilbert's hazel eyes were kind of nice to look at. Her heart gave a funny little beat. But then the hurt from that awful day two years ago came back to her as if it had been yesterday. Gilbert had called her "Carrots" and made her feel ashamed in front of the whole school. She would never forgive him!

"No," she said coldly. "I shall never be friends with you, Gilbert Blythe."

"All right," he shouted as he jumped back into his boat. "I'll never ask you to be friends again, Anne Shirley!"

As Anne watched Gilbert pull away from the landing, she felt a pang of

regret. She wished that she had answered him differently. He *had* hurt her feelings terribly, but—

She decided that the best thing to do was to have a good cry.

Halfway up the path, she met Jane and Diana rushing back to the pond. They had found no one at Diana's house to help and were in a blind panic.

"Oh, Anne," said Diana, throwing her arms around her friend and weeping. "We thought you were dead and that we were murderers for making you be Elaine. How did you escape?"

"I climbed onto one of the bridge stumps," said Anne wearily. "Then Gilbert Blythe came rowing along and brought me to land."

"Oh, how lovely of him! That's so romantic!" said Jane.

"I don't ever want to hear the word *romantic* again," said Anne, back to her old self. "It's nothing but trouble. We've lost your father's boat, Diana, and I

have a feeling we won't be allowed to row on the pond anymore."

That feeling proved exactly right when the grown-ups in the Cuthbert and Barry households found out what had happened that afternoon.

"Will you *ever* have any sense, Anne?" groaned Marilla.

"Oh yes, I think I will," said Anne. "I think my chances of becoming sensible are better now than ever."

"I don't see how," said Marilla.

"I learned a valuable lesson today," explained Anne. "I realized that there is probably no use trying to be romantic in Avonlea. It was probably easy enough in King Arthur's court hundreds of years ago, but romance is not appreciated nowadays. Not even by me."

Matthew, who had been sitting quietly in the corner, waited until Marilla had left the room. Then he whispered, "Don't give up *all* your romance, Anne. A little of it is a good thing. Keep a little of it."

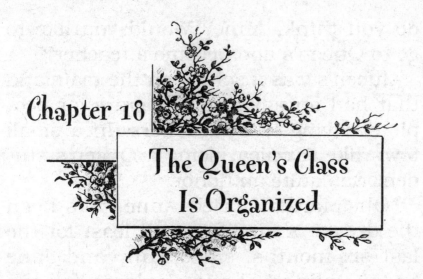

Chapter 18

The Queen's Class Is Organized

One late afternoon in November, Anne came home from Diana's house to find Marilla waiting for her in the kitchen.

"Miss Stacy was here while you were out," said Marilla mysteriously. "She was talking about you."

"What did she say?" asked Anne.

"She's organizing a group of her most advanced students to study for The Entrance Exam to Queen's, and wanted to know if we were interested for you. What do you think, Anne? Would you like to go to Queen's and become a teacher?"

Queen's was a school on the mainland that had an advanced program for people studying to be teachers. In a small town like Avonlea, being a Queen's student was quite an honor.

"Oh, Marilla!" cried Anne. "It's been the dream of my life! Or at least for the last six months, since Ruby and Jane began talking about studying for the test. I would love to be a teacher. But wouldn't Queen's be too expensive?"

"When Matthew and I decided to adopt you, we agreed to take good care of you," said Marilla. "That includes getting you the best education we can. You can join the Queen's class if you like."

"Oh, Marilla, thank you." Anne threw her arms around Marilla's waist. "I am so grateful to you and Matthew. I'll work as hard as I possibly can. I warn you not to expect much in geometry. But in all the rest, I think I can hold my own."

The Queen's study group included Anne, Josie Pye, Ruby Gillis, and, among others, Gilbert Blythe. They stayed an extra hour after school every day to study with Miss Stacy. It was a terrific challenge, and Anne enjoyed every minute of it except for one thing: Her bosom friend Diana was not in the class.

Ever since the night when Minnie May was sick, Anne and Diana had never been separated in anything. That first afternoon of the Queen's class, watching Diana leave school without her was almost too much for Anne to bear.

"Oh, Marilla, I really felt that I had tasted the bitterness of death when I saw Diana go home that night," said Anne later. "But it *is* rather exciting to be in the Queen's class. Everyone in it is looking forward to great things."

"What is Gilbert Blythe going to be?" asked Marilla.

"I have no idea *what* ambition Gilbert

Blythe has in life," said Anne scornfully, "or if he has any ambitions at all."

There was now open rivalry between Anne and Gilbert. Both were determined to be the best student in class. Gilbert was just as smart as Anne was. None of the other students even tried to compete with either of them.

Ever since Anne had refused his friendship by the pond, Gilbert had acted as if he didn't even know Anne was alive, outside of their competition for grades. He laughed and joked with all the other boys and girls. Although Anne told herself that it didn't matter, it hurt her to be ignored.

Her old anger toward Gilbert had vanished after that day at the pond. If she could do it over again, and differently, she would. But she would never have that chance. Nobody—not even Diana— knew how sorry she was and how much she wished she had not been so proud and awful to Gilbert that day.

That winter passed in a haze of snowy

sunshine and study. Soon spring returned, and school was over for another year. Anne put her books in a trunk in the attic, promising to not even look at them until fall. She and Diana spent a lovely summer practically living outdoors.

In the fall, Miss Stacy found all her students eager to work again. Especially the Queen's class, who had something waiting for them at the end of the term that made them all shake in their boots

with terror. It was known as The Entrance, an exam that would decide who went to Queen's and who did not.

For Anne, the joy of a new school year was mixed with sadness. Only a few months lay between her and The Entrance, gateway to a new and exciting adventure. But getting into Queen's would mean leaving Avonlea, and Matthew, Marilla, and Diana. It was too painful and confusing to think about, so Anne threw herself into her studies as never before.

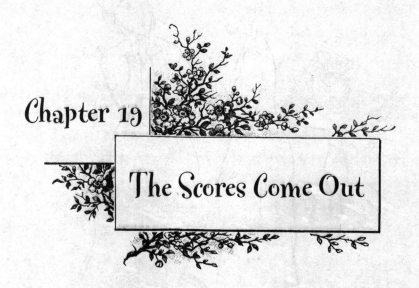

Chapter 19

The Scores Come Out

Anne was growing so fast that Marilla was shocked one day standing next to her, to find that the girl was taller than *she* was.

"My, how you've grown!" she said, almost not believing it. A sigh followed the words. Marilla felt a strange sadness over Anne's height. The child she had grown to love had disappeared somehow, and here was this tall, serious-eyed girl of fifteen.

That night, Matthew came home and

found Marilla crying, all by herself, in the living room.

"I was just thinking about Anne," she explained. "She'll probably be away from us next winter. I'll miss her terribly."

"She'll come home often," comforted Matthew.

"But it won't be the same as having her here all the time," said Marilla, enjoying her gloomy mood. "But men don't understand these things!"

There were other changes in Anne, too. For one thing, she had grown much quieter. Perhaps she dreamed more than before, but she certainly talked less.

"You don't chatter half as much as you used to, or use such big words," Marilla said one day. "What has come over you?"

Anne just laughed and blushed a little. She just didn't feel like talking as much as she used to.

"You've got only two months left before The Entrance," said Marilla. "Do you think you'll be able to pass?"

Anne shivered. "I don't know," she said. "Sometimes I think I will. But then I get horribly afraid. I wish it were all over, Marilla. It haunts me. Sometimes I wake up in the night and wonder what I'll do if I don't pass."

"Why, just go to school next year and try again," said Marilla cheerfully.

"I don't know if I'd have the heart for it," said Anne. "It would be awful to fail, especially if Gil—I mean if the others passed."

With the end of June came the end of school. Miss Stacy was leaving to take a teaching job far away. Anne and Diana walked home on the final day of school with tears flowing down their faces.

"Doesn't it seem like the end of everything?" asked Diana tearfully.

"You shouldn't feel half as bad as I do," cried Anne. "You'll be back again next winter. But I guess I've left our dear old school forever—if I'm lucky enough to pass The Entrance."

"It won't be the same," said Diana, drying her eyes. "We sure had jolly times, Anne. It's terrible to think that they're all over."

The next week, Anne went to the mainland to study extra hard. Then she and the rest of the group took The Entrance, which took two whole days!

Anne returned to Green Gables on a beautiful Friday evening. Diana was there to greet her. They acted as if Anne had been away for years.

"Oh, how good it is to be back!" cried Anne. "Green Gables is the loveliest spot in the whole world."

"How did you do?" asked Diana.

"Geometry was the only thing I had trouble with, but I have a feeling that I might have passed that, too," said Anne. "But we won't know anything until the scores come out in the newspaper in two weeks. We'll just have to wait and see."

"I just hope I got one of the top

scores," said Anne after a pause. By that she meant that she hoped she had scored better than Gilbert Blythe.

Every time she had even glimpsed Gilbert's face, it had made her work harder to get the best score possible. She knew that her whole school was waiting to see which of them had scored higher. Some students were even betting money on one or the other.

But Anne had another, more noble reason to score high: for Matthew and Marilla. She was so thankful for all they had done for her. Besides, Matthew had told her that he thought she would get the highest score on the whole island. She didn't want to let him down.

Anne thought that it would be foolish to even dream of scoring in the top ten, but she hoped she would. Then she could see Matthew's kindly brown eyes beam with pride in what she had done.

When three weeks had passed and the scores still were not in the evening paper, Anne was so nervous that she felt as if she might never eat or sleep again. Next evening, she was sitting in the window, trying to let the beautiful summer night make her forget about The Entrance when she saw Diana come flying down the road. Anne knew at once that Diana had The Entrance scores.

She was almost dizzy and her head started to ache. She could not move a step. It seemed like an hour before Diana rushed down the hall and burst into the room without even knocking.

"Anne, you passed!" she cried, waving the paper in the air. "You and Gilbert are tied for first place!"

Anne managed to make her shaking hands work well enough to take the paper and look for herself. There it was, her name, on top of a list of two hundred students.

"I'm dazzled inside!" she said. "I want to say a hundred things, but I just can't find words to say anything."

Diana smiled back at Anne, exhausted from her long run.

"Excuse me Diana," said Anne when she had settled down a bit. "I must go out in the field and tell Matthew."

As luck would have it, Marilla and Matthew were standing together, talking with Mrs. Rachel Lynde, when the girls reached the hayfield.

"Oh, Matthew," cried Anne. "Marilla! I passed and I'm first—or one of the first!"

"Well now, I've always said it," said Matthew. "I knew you could beat 'em all."

"You've done pretty well, I must say," said Marilla, trying to hide her pride from Mrs. Lynde's critical eye. But Mrs. Lynde seemed even more excited.

"She sure has done well, and I won't be shy about saying it," she hollered. "You're a credit to your friends, Anne, that's what, and we're all proud of you."

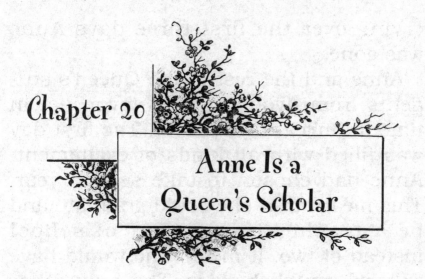

Chapter 20

Anne Is a Queen's Scholar

Anne's summer flew by. There was a lot to do to get ready for Queen's School. She had to have new clothes and school supplies. She tried to spend as much time as she could with Diana, Matthew, and Marilla, so she might not miss them as terribly when she went away.

The day finally came when Anne had to leave for school. She had a tearful good-bye with Diana, and a tearless one with Marilla. Marilla did all of her crying over the first three days Anne was gone.

Anne and the rest of the Queen's students from Avonlea got to town just in time to hurry off to school. The first day was filled with all kinds of excitement. Anne had chosen to take second year. This meant that she could graduate and be a teacher in one year of school instead of two. It meant she would have to work much harder. The only other Avonlea student in the second-year program was Gilbert Blythe.

At first, Anne felt very lonely among so many strangers. So lonely, in fact, that it was actually pleasant to look across the room and see Gilbert Blythe. She still didn't speak to him, of course, but when one is among strangers, a familiar face is a comfort, no matter whose it is. Besides, she knew that he would want to get better grades than she did, and that would make her work harder than she might have otherwise.

"Just look at him," she thought. "I'll bet right now he's thinking about trying

to win the gold medal for best in class instead of me. I'll show him."

But then, a softer thought popped into her head. "Why, I never noticed what a fine chin he has." This thought made her feel strange, so she tried to concentrate on feeling lonely again.

If Anne thought she was homesick that day in school, it was nothing compared with her feelings the first night at Queen's. As she sat alone in her little boardinghouse room, it was all she could do to keep herself from crying.

"I won't cry," she said to herself. "It's silly and weak. I must think of something funny to cheer myself up. But nothing is funny. I might as well go ahead and be miserable. It's more fun when one is this sad."

The only thing that saved Anne from crying all night was a visit from Josie Pye, who was at Queen's with her.

"You've been crying," teased Josie. "Some people have so little self control. I

couldn't possibly be homesick. This big town is too jolly after pokey old Avonlea."

Anne almost laughed. Josie had been a snooty girl at home, and being at Queen's had done nothing to improve her personality so far. Anne couldn't decide whether she would have rather stayed lonely and miserable all by herself. But she brightened when she heard what else Josie had to say.

"Did you hear?" Josie said. "Queen's is giving out an Avery scholarship this year!"

Anne's ears perked up. The Avery scholarship was awarded to the student who received the best scores in English. The prize was free tuition to Redmond College for all four years! Anne knew that she had as good a chance to win it as Gilbert Blythe or anyone else.

"Imagine me going to college!" thought Anne, "How proud Matthew and Marilla would be of me then."

Suddenly the old spark was back in Anne's eye. She sat and planned her strategy for winning the Avery scholarship. Even though she probably hadn't meant to do so, Josie Pye had cheered Anne completely.

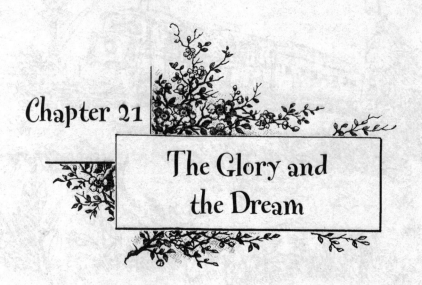

Chapter 21

The Glory and the Dream

Over time, Anne's homesickness faded, mostly because she often went home on weekends. On those Friday nights, most of the Avonlea students would take the train home together. They were usually met by Diana and other young people at the station, and they would walk together in the crisp autumn air toward the friendly, twinkling lights of Avonlea. Anne thought of those happy evenings as the best and

dearest hours in the whole week.

When winter came, Anne and the others stopped going home on weekends so they could study even harder. Everyone agreed that Anne and Gilbert were both in the running to win the Avery scholarship. Their rivalry was as strong as ever. But the old bitterness was gone.

In fact, sometimes when Anne saw Gilbert out in the town with another girl from school, she couldn't help thinking that it would be nice to have a friend like him to joke with and talk about studies and ambitions. Gilbert had ambitions. But her girlfriends, like Ruby Gillis and Josie Pye, didn't seem like the kind of people you could talk with about such things.

It wasn't as if she had a crush on Gilbert or anything. Anne hardly ever thought about boys at all. When she did, it was only that they seemed as if they might be fun friends. But Anne had gathered a nice little circle of girlfriends at Queen's. Besides, she hardly had any time for anything but studying anyway.

Spring came. In Avonlea, mayflowers were peeking out in lush green fields. But at Queen's School, all the students could think about were final exams.

"It doesn't seem possible that the school year is almost over," said Anne one night. "It feels as if yesterday was our first day here at Queen's and yet here we are, about to begin final exams tomorrow morning! I don't know whether to worry about exams or run outside and admire the green buds in the trees."

"I've lost seven pounds just this week worrying about exams," said Jane Andrews. "It would be so awful if I failed after spending so much money to come here!"

"Well, I don't care," said Josie Pye. "My father is rich. If I fail, he'll just send me here again next year. Oh, Anne, someone heard Professor Tremaine say that he thinks Gilbert Blythe is going to win the medal for best in class, and Emily May is going to win the Avery scholarship."

"That may make me feel bad tomorrow, Josie," laughed Anne, "but just now I feel that as long as I know the violets are coming out all purple in the little hollow at home behind Green Gables, it's not that big a deal whether I win the Avery scholarship or not. I've done my best. Let's not talk about exams anymore."

The morning the final-exam scores were to be posted, Anne and Jane walked toward the school. Jane was smiling. She would be happy just to pass, and expected that she had done that. Anne, on the other hand, was a bundle of nerves.

"I'm afraid I have no hope of winning the Avery," she admitted. "Everyone thinks that Emily is going to get it. I can't go up to the bulletin board and read the scores myself. I'll go straight to the girls' locker room. You go read the scores and report them to me, whether they're good or bad."

Jane promised to do so but, as it turned out, there was no need. When they got to the school building, they found a hallway full of boys carrying Gilbert Blythe on their shoulders, yelling, "Hooray for Blythe, gold medalist!"

For one moment, Anne felt a sickening pang of defeat. She had failed and Gil had won. Matthew would be so disappointed.

Just then somebody else called out, "Three cheers for Anne Shirley, winner of the Avery!"

"Oh, Anne," said Jane as they escaped

into the girls' locker room. "Oh, Anne. Isn't it splendid? I'm so proud!"

Suddenly, a mob of happy girls surrounded Anne. They thumped her shoulders and shook her hands. As they pushed and pulled and hugged her, she managed to whisper to Jane, "Matthew and Marilla will be so pleased! I must write the news home right away!"

At graduation, Matthew and Marilla were there with eyes for only one student, the Avery winner—a tall girl with beautiful red hair and starry eyes.

"I reckon you're glad that we kept her, Marilla," whispered Matthew as Anne crossed the stage to receive her diploma.

"It's not the first time I've been glad," said Marilla. "You do like to say 'I told you so,' don't you, Matthew Cuthbert?"

Chapter 22

Home Again

Anne went home to Avonlea with Matthew and Marilla the very next day. She hadn't visited since April, and couldn't wait another minute. Diana rushed to Green Gables as soon as she heard them coming down the road.

"Oh, Diana, it's so good to see you again," said Anne, "and it's so good to be back at Green Gables. Everything looks and smells so beautiful here. I'm so tired. I'm going to spend at least two hours

tomorrow lying out on the orchard grass and thinking about absolutely nothing."

"You've done so well," said Diana. "I guess you won't be teaching since you won the Avery."

"That's right," said Anne. "I'm going to Redmond College next year. Everyone has good news. We all passed the exams—even Josie Pye. Isn't it exciting?"

"Yes," agreed Diana. "But did you hear about Gilbert Blythe? He can't afford to go to college, so he accepted the teaching job right here at our little school."

For a moment, Anne felt something like sadness. She had thought that Gilbert would be going to Redmond, too. What would she do without their rivalry? Would she do as well without her friend, the enemy?

It struck Anne the next morning that Matthew did not look at all well. He was much grayer than he had been a year ago.

"Marilla," she said when he had gone out to the fields. "Is Matthew feeling well?"

"No, he isn't," said Marilla, sounding worried. "He's had a few real bad spells with his heart. I've been real worried about him. Maybe now that you're home, he'll take a little time off. You always cheer him up."

"You're not looking so well either, Marilla," warned Anne. "Now that I'm home, you should take it easy while I do the work around here."

"It's not the work," said Marilla, smiling at her grown-up girl. "It's my head. I get terrible headaches now. Dr. Spencer has arranged for me to go see a special eye doctor next month."

Later that day, Anne found Matthew out in the field. "You've been working too hard today," she scolded gently. "Why don't you take it easier?"

"I can't seem to," he said. "I've worked hard all my life. I like it. I'm just getting old, that's all."

"If I had been that boy you sent for, I could be helping you now in so many ways," said Anne.

"I'd rather have you than a dozen boys," said Matthew, patting her hand. "It wasn't a boy who took the Avery scholarship, was it? It was a girl—*my girl*—my girl who I'm proud of."

Anne smiled as she watched him walk into the barn. She gazed out over the beautiful flower-covered hills. She thought of her two parents who loved her and her beautiful home. Forever afterward, Anne remembered that lovely, peaceful evening. It was the last night before sorrow touched her life; and no one is ever quite the same after that cold touch has been laid upon it.

Chapter 23

The Reaper Whose Name Is Death

"Matthew—Matthew—what's the matter? Matthew, are you sick?"

Anne heard Marilla speaking those sharp, alarm-filled words. She ran into the room and looked past Marilla to see Matthew standing in the doorway clutching a piece of paper in his hand. His face was a terrible ashen gray. She sprang across the kitchen to his side at the same time Marilla did. They were too late. By the time they reached Matthew, he had collapsed in the doorway.

"He's fainted!" gasped Marilla. "Anne, run and get Martin! He's in the barn!"

Martin, the hired man, went for the doctor right away, stopping at Orchard Slope first for help. Mrs. Lynde was the first to arrive. She checked Matthew's pulse, putting her head on his chest to listen. When she looked up at Marilla, her eyes were filled with tears.

"Oh, Marilla," she said sadly, "I don't think we can do anything for him."

When the doctor arrived, he said that Matthew had died instantly of a heart attack, probably caused by a sudden shock. When they looked at the piece of paper he had been holding, they knew the doctor was right.

The paper was an announcement that the Abbey Bank had failed. Matthew and Marilla's savings had been wiped out! They were broke. The shock had been too much for Matthew's weak heart.

The news spread quickly through the little town. All day, people came to Green Gables with small gifts, food, and kind words. Diana offered to stay the night.

"Thank you," said Anne, "But I have to be alone. I haven't even cried yet. Half the time I can't believe Matthew is dead. The other half, it seems as if he's been dead a long time and I've had this terrible dull ache ever since."

Anne hoped that she would cry as soon as she was alone. But she didn't. When she woke late in the night, the facts of the day swept over her in a wave of sorrow. She could see Matthew standing near the barn and saying with a smile, "My girl—my girl who I'm proud of."

Then the tears came in a flood. Marilla came up the stairs to comfort her.

"There, there, dearie," she said softly. "It can't bring him back. But I know just how you feel. He'd always been such a good and kind brother to me."

"Oh, Marilla," said Anne. "What will we do without him?"

"We've got each other, Anne," Marilla said. "I don't know what I'd do if you'd never come. Anne, I know that I've been strict with you sometimes, but you mustn't think I don't love you as much as Matthew did. It's not easy for me to speak from my heart, but I want to tell you: I love you as if you were my flesh and blood, and you've been my greatest joy since you've come to Green Gables."

Two days later, they buried Matthew near the fields he had planted and the

orchards he had loved so dearly.

In the days that passed, Anne began to visit with Diana again—and sometimes even smile and laugh. But Anne was often sad and lonely for Matthew. She became sadder still when she thought of how lonely Marilla would be when she went off to college.

"What a nice-looking young fellow Gilbert Blythe is," said Marilla one day. "I saw him in church on Sunday. He seemed so tall and manly. He looks a lot like his father did at his age. John Blythe was a nice boy. We were real good friends. People used to call him my beau."

Anne looked up with interest.

"I never knew that," she exclaimed. "What happened between you?"

"We had a quarrel and I wouldn't forgive him for it. I meant to after a while, but I was too sulky and angry and I wanted to punish him at first. He never came back. I always felt—well, rather sorry. I've always kind of wished I had forgiven him when I had the chance."

"So you've had a bit of romance in your life, too," said Anne softly.

"Yes, I suppose you might call it that," said Marilla with a little smile. "You wouldn't think so to look at me, would you? Everybody has forgotten about me and John Blythe. I'd even forgotten myself. But it all came back to me when I saw Gilbert last Sunday."

Chapter 24

The Bend in the Road

The next afternoon, Anne returned from the Barry house to find Marilla at the kitchen table, leaning her head on her hand. Something in the way she was sitting struck a chill in Anne's heart. She had never seen Marilla look so down.

"Is it one of your headaches, Marilla? Are you very tired?"

"Yes—no—I suppose I am tired but I haven't thought about it," said Marilla.

"Did you go to the special eye doctor today, Marilla?" Anne asked her gently.

"Yes," said Marilla. "He examined my eyes. He said that if I give up sewing and reading, and if I'm careful not to cry, *and* if I wear the special glasses he's given me, then my eyes may not get any worse and my headaches will be cured. But if I don't, he says, I'll be blind in six months! Blind! Anne, just think of it."

After that shock, Anne said, "Don't think that way, Marilla! He *has* given you hope. If you're careful, you won't go blind. Your headaches might even go away."

"I don't call that much hope," said Marilla sharply. "What am I to live for if I can't read or sew or anything? I might as well be blind—or dead! Oh, let's stop talking about it, and please don't tell anybody else. I don't want a lot of busybodies around here trying to help."

That night, Anne sat in her little room with a heavy heart. How sadly things had changed since she had arrived home from Queen's. Anne felt as if she had lived a year since then. But before she went to sleep that night, she had made a decision about her future. It would be difficult, but she felt good about what she had to do.

A few days later, John Sadler, a man from Carmody, came to talk to Marilla. Afterward, Marilla joined Anne in the kitchen.

"What did Mr. Sadler want?" Anne asked.

There were tears in Marilla's eyes. "He

heard that I was going to sell Green Gables and he wants to buy it."

"Buy it? Buy Green Gables?" Anne asked, wondering if she had heard right.

"I don't know what else to do," Marilla said. "We lost every penny we had when the bank failed. Besides, I can't run this place with my eyesight going. I never thought that I'd see the day when I'd sell my home. But it looks as if the only way I can survive is to sell Green Gables and live on the money it brings. I'm sorry that you won't have a home to come to on your vacations, Anne, but I suppose you'll manage somehow." Marilla broke down and cried bitterly.

"You mustn't sell Green Gables," said Anne.

"I wish I didn't have to. But I can't stay here alone. I'd go crazy with loneliness. And I'd lose my eyesight. I know it."

"You won't have to stay here alone," said Anne. "I'll be here with you. I'm not going to Redmond."

"Not going to Redmond?" asked Marilla. "What do you mean?"

"Just what I said," replied Anne smiling. "I'm not taking the scholarship. I decided so the night after you saw the doctor. Surely you don't think that I'd leave you all alone in your trouble, after all you've done for me! Here's my plan: Mr. Barry wants to rent our farm for a year. So we won't have to worry about keeping that up, but can keep on living in the house. I'm going to teach; I've applied for the school here. I don't think I'll get it because Gilbert Blythe has already been promised the job, but I can teach at the school in Carmody. It's only a short trip each day. The rest of the time, I'll be here to read to you and keep you cheered up. You won't be lonesome at all. We'll be real cozy and happy here, you and I."

Marilla had listened like a woman in a dream.

"Oh, Anne," she said, "it would be great

if you were here, but I can't let you sacrifice yourself for me. It would be terrible."

"Nonsense!" Anne laughed merrily. "Nothing would hurt me more than giving up Green Gables. My mind is made up—I'm not going to Redmond. I'll stay here and teach. Don't worry about me."

"But you had such great ambitions!"

"I *still* have great ambitions," said Anne. "They've just changed. I'm going to be a good teacher—and I'm going to save your eyesight. When I left Queen's, my future seemed to stretch out in front of me like a straight road. Now there's a bend in that road. I don't know what lies around the bend, but I believe that the best lies there."

"You blessed girl," said Marilla. "I feel as if I should make you take that scholarship. But I know I can't. I'll make it up to you though, Anne."

When it became known around town that Anne was going to stay home and teach instead of going to college, most people thought her a fool. They didn't know about Marilla's troubles.

Mrs. Lynde didn't know about them when she came over to Green Gables one afternoon and sat on the porch with Anne and Marilla.

"Anne, I hear that you've given up going to college," she said with a smile. "I'm glad to hear it. I don't believe in young ladies going to college with men and cramming their heads full of Latin and Greek and all that nonsense."

"But I *am* going to study Latin and Greek and everything else," said Anne with a smile. "I'm going to study by mail right here at Green Gables."

Mrs. Lynde raised her hands in horror.

"Anne Shirley, you'll kill yourself!" she cried.

"No, I won't," said Anne. "I'll have lots of spare time. I'm going to teach in Carmody, you know."

"You are not," answered Mrs. Lynde. "You're going to teach right here in

Avonlea. They gave you the job last night. That's what I'm here to tell you."

"Mrs. Lynde!" cried Anne, leaping to her feet. "I thought they had given it to Gilbert Blythe!"

"They had," said Mrs. Lynde. "But as soon as Gilbert heard that you were staying, he went to them and asked them to give it to you. He's going to teach in White Sands instead. Of course he only did it for you, because he heard that you wanted to stay here. I think it was awfully nice of him, don't you?"

"I don't think I should take it," said Anne. "I don't want him to sacrifice himself for me."

"You can't do anything about it now," said Mrs. Lynde. "He's signed a contract with the White Sands School."

The next morning, Anne went out and put fresh flowers on Matthew's grave. On her way back, she stopped to look at all the beauty around her.

"Dear old world," she said softly. "You are lovely, and I'm glad to be alive in you."

Soon afterward, she passed the Blythe home. A tall young man was just letting himself out of the gate, whistling. It was Gilbert, and the whistle died on his lips as he saw Anne. He tipped his hat to her, but he would have passed on in silence if she hadn't stopped and held out her hand.

"Gilbert," she said with red cheeks, "I want to thank you for giving up the school for me. It was very good of you."

Gilbert took her hand eagerly. "It was nothing," he said. "I'm glad to be able to help. Are we going to be friends after this? Have you finally forgiven me?"

"I forgave you that day at the pond—I just didn't know it then. What a silly goose I was! I may as well make a full confession: I have been sorry ever since."

"We are going to be the best of friends," said Gilbert. "We were born to be friends. We've avoided our fate for too long. You're going to keep up your studies, aren't you? So am I. Come on. I'll walk you home."

Marilla gave Anne a curious look when she came into the kitchen.

"Who was that you were talking to, Anne?"

"Gilbert Blythe," said Anne, surprised to find herself blushing.

"I didn't know that you two were such good friends to be standing for half an hour at the gate, talking," said Marilla with a dry smile.

"We haven't been," said Anne. "We've

been good enemies. But not any more. Was it really half an hour? It seemed like just a few minutes. But you see, we have five years' lost time to make up."

That night, Anne sat happily in her little gable window. Her horizons had closed in since she left Queen's. But if the path before her feet was to be narrow, at least she knew that flowers of quiet happiness would bloom along it—and there would always be the bend in the road.

"God's in His heaven, all's right with the world," she whispered softly.

The End

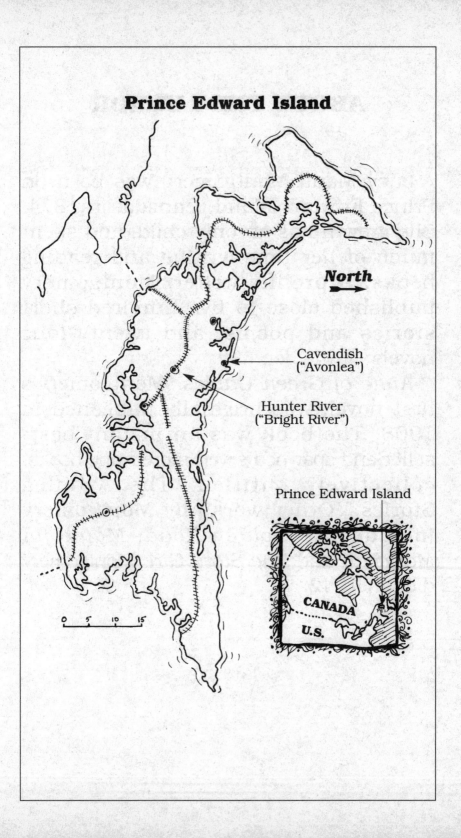

Prince Edward Island

North →

Cavendish
("Avonlea")

Hunter River
("Bright River")

Prince Edward Island

0 5 10 15

CANADA

U.S.

ABOUT THE AUTHOR

Lucy Maud Montgomery was born on Prince Edward Island, Canada, in 1874. She grew up as an only child, and spent much of her time writing and reading books. A prolific writer, Montgomery published close to five hundred short stories and poems, and twenty-four novels.

Anne of Green Gables, Montgomery's first novel, was originally published in 1908. The book was an instant bestseller and spawned seven more Anne books, collectively entitled "The Avonlea Stories." Other works by Montgomery include *The Golden Road*, *Magic for Marigold*, and *The Story Girl*. Montgomery died in 1942.

Treasury of Illustrated Classics™

Adventures of Huckleberry Finn
The Adventures of Robin Hood
The Adventures of Sherlock Holmes
The Adventures of Tom Sawyer
Alice in Wonderland
Anne of Green Gables
Black Beauty
The Call of the Wild
Gulliver's Travels
Heidi
Jane Eyre
The Legend of Sleepy Hollow
& Rip Van Winkle
A Little Princess
Little Women
Moby Dick
Oliver Twist
Peter Pan
Rebecca of Sunnybrook Farm
Robinson Crusoe
The Secret Garden
Swiss Family Robinson
Treasure Island
20,000 Leagues Under the Sea
The Wizard of Oz